Nick Hornby's best-known books are *High
Fidelity*, *About a Boy* and *Fever Pitch*. All three
have been made into films. His most recent
book is *A Long Way Down*.

All royalties from the Irish sales of the Open
Door series go to a charity of the author's
choice. *Not a Star* royalties go to The
TreeHouse Trust, Woodside Avenue, London.

NEW ISLAND Open Door

NOT A STAR
Published 2006
by New Island
2 Brookside
Dundrum Road
Dublin 14

www.newisland.ie

Copyright © 2006 Nick Hornby

The right of Nick Hornby to be identified as the author of this work has been asserted by him in accordance with the Copyright, Designs and Patents Act, 1988

A CIP catalogue record for this book is available from the British Library

ISBN 1 905494 05 X

New Island receives financial assistance from
The Arts Council (An Chomhairle Ealaíon), Dublin, Ireland.

This book is sold subject to the condition that it shall not, by way of trade or otherwise, be lent, resold, hired out, or otherwise circulated in any form of binding or cover other than that in which it is published and without a similar condition, including this condition, being imposed on the subsequent purchaser.

Typeset by New Island
Printed in Ireland by ColourBooks
Cover design by Artmark

3 5 4

Dear Reader,

On behalf of myself and the other contributing authors, I would like to welcome you to the fifth Open Door series. We hope that you enjoy the books and that reading becomes a lasting pleasure in your life.

Warmest wishes,

Patricia Scanlan.

Patricia Scanlan
Series Editor

I found out that my son was the star of a porn film when Karen from two doors down dropped an envelope through our letter box. Inside the envelope was a video and a little note. The note said:

Dear Lynn,

I'm not in the habit of dropping smutty films through people's letter boxes. But I thought you and Frank might be interested in this one! It's not mine, I should add! Carl was at a mate's house on Friday night after they had been out drinking. His mate put this tape on – you know what they are like! And Carl recognised Someone You Might Know. He couldn't stop laughing. I had no idea! Does he get this from his dad? You have kept it quiet if he does!

Love,
Karen

It had to be her, didn't it? It had to be bloody Karen. She's a nurse at the hospital. So she knows everyone and everything. And whatever she finds out, she passes on to whoever is standing around. It doesn't matter whether it is their business or not, or if they are interested or not. She knew Dave had had the snip about ten minutes before I did. Half the town knew about it five minutes later. Everything has to go through her. So it would have to be her son that saw Mark's film. It couldn't have been any other way. It's the law around here.

I was the only one in when I picked the envelope up off the doormat. Dave wasn't back from work. Mark plays five-a-side after college on Wednesdays. I opened the envelope at the kitchen table, read the note and then looked at the video. It was called … Listen, if I am going to tell this story, I will have to use some words that might offend you. But if I don't say them, you won't get any sense of the shock I felt. The film was called *Meet the Fuckers*. There was a picture of Mark on the cover. He was standing behind a woman with huge boobs. And he had his hands over them so you couldn't see everything.

My knees started to shake. I

couldn't stand up. I could hardly breathe. I hadn't seen the film then, so I could still imagine that my son didn't really do very much. I could believe that he just stood behind topless women, covering their boobs with his hands. I think that for a moment I told myself Mark was just being a gentleman. There was this poor girl, caught with no blouse. She was thankful that Mark was there to hide her shame … You know what it's like when you have kids. You will only believe the worst of them when you have no other choice.

I found it impossible to get my head around it. Mark! I thought. My Mark! Mark who used to sit at the kitchen table trying to do his English homework. He found it so difficult that he chewed his way through his Biro, night after night. At first, I didn't know why that memory made the video seem so hard to believe. Millions of people must take their clothes off for a living. Every single one of them probably found their English homework a bit of a struggle. Or is that just me making excuses? Could you be top of your class in English and then go on to star in a film called *Meet the Fuckers*? It's hard to imagine, isn't it?

But then I worked out why the Biro-chewing didn't seem to fit with the career in porn. Mark is … well, he has never been the star of anything. He has been trying to get a leisure and tourism diploma so he can get a job in a sports centre. But he is finding the studying hard. We are worried that it might be too much for him. We are afraid that he might have set his sights too high. Anyway, when I saw him on the cover of that video, I realised we had got used to the idea of thinking of him as – I don't know. Not special. I mean, he is special because he is our son. But it seemed to me that the two words I had said to him most over the last few years were "Never mind". School reports, exam results, job applications, football trials, girlfriends: "Never mind", "Never mind", "Never mind".

I haven't really seen any porn films. Only what was on TV when we were on holiday in Spain, when we found that German cable channel. But say someone had told me that Mark had appeared in one. And say they asked me to guess what part he played. I would have said that he was the husband who discovered his wife in bed with the window-cleaner or something like that. I would never have guessed that he would be on the cover. Sad, isn't it, the way you sort of give up on your kids?

So it was like I had to get used to this whole new life. A new life in which Mark had something that marked him out. A life where he had something that made him different to everyone else. I had no idea what that something was, though. That was the next big shock.

2

I know this sounds funny, but I probably hadn't thought about Mark's penis since the day he was born. I mean, I didn't even think about it very much then. But that was the last time it actually sort of meant something to me. Because on the day he was born, his penis was who he was – if you know what I mean. The midwife held him up and said, "It's a little boy." And I looked, and it was. So Mark was Mark, and not Olivia. That is who he would have been if he didn't have one. And after that … Well, I washed him and everything, until he was old enough to do it himself. And then that was it. Our relationship was over. When he started seeing girls, Dave and I would wonder whether he was sleeping with them. But I never thought about that actual part of him. I told Dave to talk to him about contraception and the rest of it. And when I thought about his sex life … Well, I tried not to.

Once, when he was seventeen or so, I walked into his bedroom on a Thursday afternoon. And he was there with Lisa, his girlfriend at the time. They weren't naked or anything. But they weren't doing their homework either. His hands were all over her. I just walked out again. And I got Dave to talk to him later. He told him what would happen if he got someone pregnant, what it would cost him. I left Dave to work that bit out, because –

never mind, never mind – I couldn't. But I never said anything. I wished I hadn't seen what I saw, though. It was as if I had walked in on my mum and dad doing something. I suppose someone has written a book about sex and the family. It is obviously an important and difficult subject. But the trouble is, you wouldn't want to read it, would you?

I had to think about all of it when I put the video on. I had to think about Mark's penis and sex and the family – everything. I didn't watch it all. I couldn't. And it wasn't just because Mark was in it or because it was filthy. It was also rubbish, cheap and vulgar and depressing. It was like a naked version of an old seventies sitcom. The girl with the big breasts, for example, was meant to be French. Of course, she said, "Ooh la la." It was about all she did say. But I saw enough to understand why Mark was on the cover. It was the biggest one I'd ever seen. OK, I haven't seen many. But you see them around more than you used to, don't you? You see them in films. Some of the girls in work have posters up. And Dave is not the only man I've ever slept with. And I can honestly say that the ones I've seen were all pretty much the same size, give or take. Mark's, though … It looked like it didn't belong to him. It looked like it was a special effect. In fact, the only reason I knew for sure it was real was that no one would put Mark in a film if it wasn't for his thing. He can't act to save his life. You could hardly hear what he was saying because he mumbled so badly. And it's not even as if he looks like Tom Cruise. He is nice looking, I think. But no one would go to all the trouble of making an enormous penis for him. Mark was special after all. We would never have to say "Never mind" about that.

You're probably thinking to yourself, "Hold on. She really had no idea? Is she blind or stupid?" And as the film was going on I wondered if I was. The girls on the screen rolled their eyes in disbelief. (That wasn't all they did. But there was a lot of the eye-rolling, and I was grateful for it.) So they rolled their eyes, and I tried to work out whether I'd missed any clues the last few years.

And the first thing I remembered was that he didn't like taking communal showers. There had been a thing about it in school. In the end we had had to write a note to his PE teacher. Neither of us had sat him down to ask him what the problem was. He had just told us that he didn't like them, that he felt funny about them. Dave was even worried that he might be queer. But we had already found a couple of girly magazines under his bed, so that idea didn't make much sense.

And then I started to think about his thing with trousers. He has always preferred baggy ones. He has never worn jeans or anything like that. And we have always teased him a bit because he has ended up looking so straight. He has got more suits than any normal twenty-three-year-old. He buys them in the Oxfam shop and places like that. And he has got endless pairs of what my mum would call "slacks". You know, those trousers with creases in them, made out of flannel or whatever. He always said that other kids were all scruffy and dirty. He said no one knew how to dress properly any more. But now I could see that he had invented his look to get himself out of a tight spot, as it were. His clothes never seemed to fit with the rest of his personality. They didn't go with the music he liked or the friends he hung around with. We could never really understand it. But that was just because we didn't have all the information we needed.

Oh, plus: he stopped me buying his pants. He was clever about it, because he said I didn't understand about stuff like that, pants and socks and vests. But looking back, I can see it was the pants part of it all that he was worried about. He didn't like slips much, and he didn't like boxers. He would only wear something he calls "boxer briefs". They are sort of like trunks but with a pouch to put it in. They look a bit show-offy, the sort of thing a male stripper might wear. Dave went back to thinking he was gay for a little while. But Mark had moved away from girly mags and on to real girls by this time. And it seemed to me that Mark was going to a lot of trouble just to prove he was straight if he wasn't. We didn't waste a lot of time puzzling it all out. He just had his quirks; that was all. Who doesn't?

I turned the video off and sat there for a moment. Dave was due back any minute. Mark would be in after he had had a drink with his five-a-side team. I didn't know what I was going to say to either of them. Maybe I didn't have to say anything. Maybe I could just march up to bloody Karen's house and give her the film back. I could tell her that if she ever breathed a word to anybody about Mark's thing, I would bash her over the head with it. But in my heart of hearts I knew it was too late.

3

Dave came in to find me sitting on the sofa staring at a blank TV screen.

"You all right?" he said.

"I've just had a bit of a shock," I told him.

"What's up?" He sat down with me, took my hand, and looked at me. He was frightened. And just for a moment, I could see that finding out your son had a huge penis was not the same as finding out you had cancer. So I tried to smile.

"Oh, it's nothing. Really. It's just …"

I reached down to the floor, picked up the video case, and gave it to him. He laughed.

"What?" I said.

"Who gave you that?"

"Karen from two doors down."

"I can see why. That's funny," said Dave.

"What's funny?"

"He looks just like him, doesn't he? Have you shown him?"

"Not yet. He's at football. Dave …" I took a deep breath. "It is Mark."

He looked at me. Then he looked at the video. Then he looked at me again.

"How do you mean?"

I put my hands up as if to say, "I don't know an easier way to explain it."

"Mark?" said Dave

"Yeah," I replied.

"In this film?"

"Yeah."

"Doing what?" he asked.

I put my hands up again. Though this time, I meant, "Well, what do people normally do in porn films?"

"Why?" he asked.

"You will have to ask him that."

"But, I mean … Why would they choose Mark? He's not … He can't …"

"Dave," I said. "Our son has the biggest … thing I've ever seen."

We had a talk then, about the pants and the showers and the rest of it. It was like one of those conversations you hear on *ER* or something like that. You know, "How did we miss the signs? How could we be so blind?" Except in *ER* they are usually talking about heroin addiction or prostitution. Those are more important things. And the signs they are talking about aren't anywhere near as obvious. They have more of an excuse for their blindness.

"He has been hiding it," said Dave.

And that was the first time I actually laughed.

"He has, though, hasn't he? For years and years. Bloody hell."

"What did you want him to do?" I said.

"I don't know. He could have talked to us."

"Could he? He couldn't have talked to me."

"Why not?" asked Dave.

"I'm his mother. He is not going to tell me stuff like that. I wouldn't have let him, to be honest."

"So it was my job?"

"It was nobody's job. What could you have done? Ask him every few months how it's coming along? It was up to him, Dave. And he didn't want to … you know – share the load."

The trouble is, you can't help it. Everything you say sounds dirty, without you wanting it to. So you end up cracking jokes about your own son's private parts. It seemed unhealthy but impossible to avoid. It was like breathing bad air when you live beside a motorway.

"You going to watch the film?" I asked Dave.

"No. There is no way *I* can watch that." The way he said it, with the emphasis on the "I", irritated me. It sounded like he felt he was superior in some way.

"Yeah, well, it wasn't as if I wanted to," I said.

"You did, though, didn't you? Even after you had seen his picture on the cover. You knew what you would see."

"I really didn't."

"I'm sorry," he said after a while. "It's just, you know … It just seemed like such a normal day. I didn't think I would come home to find my whole life had changed."

I didn't say anything. But I could have pointed out that most life-changing days happen without your expecting them. I have spent what seems like half my life expecting the worst. And it never happens. But on the day it does, it will knock me flat on my back anyway.

4

Mark came in at about eleven. We are usually upstairs getting ready for bed by then. But we had waited up for obvious reasons. He was surprised to see us there, sitting on the sofa watching TV.

"Is there something good on?" he asked.

Dave didn't even turn around to look at him.

"No. Not really," I said. "We just started watching this film, and now we want to see how it ends."

"I'm going to make myself a sandwich."

"OK, son."

He always comes in from the pub and makes himself a sandwich on football nights. That is why Dave had left the video on the kitchen table. That way, he would know we were on to him without us having to say anything. We didn't really have a plan after that. I suppose we thought there would be an argument, and then eventually a chat. But the next thing we heard was the front door slamming.

"Shit," said Dave. "Now what?"

"Where has he gone, do you think?" I asked.

"I don't know, do I?"

"Supposing he has left home?"

"People don't leave home like that. People don't say, 'I'm going to make myself a sandwich,' and then, bang, they're gone," Dave replied.

I didn't say anything. But from what I could tell, that is exactly what people did. You can watch the local news on just about any night of the week and see some mother talking about how her son never even said goodbye. And then there is a phone number, asking for any information.

"He might have gone round to Becca's, I suppose," Dave said.

"Shall I call her?"

"No. Give him some time. If we don't hear from him tomorrow we'll call then."

Becca was Mark's girlfriend. She had her own place a few streets away. But Mark usually didn't stay there during the week because she had a flatmate. Mark usually spent the week-ends there, when they had the place to themselves.

I hadn't thought about Becca up until

now. But once Dave had mentioned her, I couldn't help it. What …? How …? I had to stop myself. But Dave and I both went quiet at the same time. So I am sure we were thinking about the same thing.

Just then we heard the key in the lock. Mark came in and sat down in the armchair. For a moment all three of us watched the TV.

"I thought there was something wrong when you said you wanted to see how the film turned out," Mark said. It was only then I realised that we were watching Man United beating a French team. "How did you find it?" he asked.

"Karen put it through the letter box," I said.

"Karen from down the road? What was she doing with it?"

"Carl saw it round at a mate's house. He borrowed it when he recognised you."

"Have you watched it?" he asked.

"I have. Your dad hasn't."

"And I won't," Dave said, as if Mark was trying to persuade him.

"How do other people cope?" I said.

"Which other people?" Mark asked.

"Other mothers. Families. I mean, they all have mothers, don't they, porn stars?"

"I'm not a porn star," said Mark.

"What are you then?" said Dave.

"I'm not a star, am I? Stars are people like Jenna Jameson and Ron Jeremy."

"Who?"

"They are porn stars. You wouldn't know them."

"Exactly. So you could be a porn star, for all I know. You might be the

most famous porn star in Britain, and I
wouldn't have a clue," said Dave.

"You think Ron Jeremy lives at
home with his mum and dad?"

"He might do! I don't know who
Ron Jeremy is! 'Ron Jeremy'. He
sounds like exactly the sort of person
who lives with his mum and dad."

I was getting frustrated. I didn't
want to talk about where Ron Jeremy
lived. I wanted to talk to my son about
what he was doing with his life.

"How did this start?" said Dave.
"How long has it been going on? How
many films are there?"

For some reason, it hadn't occurred
to me for a moment that there might be
others.

"It started ... Well, sort of through
Becca," said Mark.

"Becca? She's a porn star too?" I
asked.

Mark sighed. "Mum. Becca works in a playgroup. You know that."

"I don't know anything any more. I don't know what she does."

"So when we went to their Christmas play last year, you thought that was a set-up, or what? Becca doesn't know anything about, you know. My other job."

"But you just said –"

"Will you let me talk? You know Becca's got a flatmate? And this flatmate has got a boyfriend who lives up North? Well, that's what he does. He makes porn films."

"Oh, well," said Dave. "That explains everything. You couldn't really help it, could you? If your girlfriend's flatmate's boyfriend makes porn films up North, you pretty much had to help him out. I mean, once you've had a phone call from him … Must be like getting a phone call from the Queen. You can't say no. And how come Becca doesn't know anything about it?"

"Because … Do you really want to go into this?"

"Yes. We both do," said Dave.

"It means talking about some pretty embarrassing stuff."

"I don't want to talk about what you do. Just how you got involved. How it happened," said Dave.

"It still means saying things you might not want to talk about," Mark replied.

"We know everything," said Dave. "Your mum has seen the film, remember."

"Yeah, well. Seeing isn't the same as talking. We could just leave it at that and never mention it again."

"How could we not mention it again?" I said. "How could we sit here night after night, eating our tea, with all that going on?"

"Not much goes on, most of the time," said Mark. "Most of the time I'm not making porn films."

"How did it happen?" said Dave.

"You've seen the film, Mum," said Mark. "So you know …" He stopped. "Oh, bloody hell. I can't talk about this to you two. I've spent the last – whatever it is, ten years, not talking to you about this."

"I've seen it," I said. "I've seen the film, and I've seen … I've seen why they would want you in it."

"OK," Mark said. "Right. Good."

He stopped again. We have never had problems talking, in our family. Usually everyone is talking at once. So these pauses and silences were something new for us. Obviously we have been talking about the wrong things all these years. It's easy to talk about nothing much.

"Becca," Dave said, as if Mark had lost his thread.

"Becca," Mark said. "When we first started going out, she had a chat with Rachel. Her flatmate."

"What sort of chat?"

"A whatever – a girly chat, sort of thing. About me. And my problem. Which had sort of become her problem too, if you catch my drift."

"Oh," Dave said.

"And Rachel passed the information on. To her boyfriend. And he phoned me. And we went on from there. And Becca never knew anything about it."

"You've never told her?" I asked.

"Of course not. You know Becca, Mum. She wouldn't understand."

"And what happens if she finds out?"

"I'll be looking for a new girlfriend, I should think."

He liked Becca. But I knew he wasn't going to end up with her, and so did he. They were already at that point where it was so comfortable that Mark was becoming uncomfortable. And there was definitely an element of Russian roulette in this. If the decision to split were taken out of his hands, he would have been grateful.

"Hold on, hold on. Rewind," said Dave. "You went on from there."

"Yeah."

"But why did you go on from there?"

"Why?" Mark repeated the question as if Dave were daft for asking it.

"Yeah. Why?"

Mark shrugged. "A bit of extra cash, obviously … And I was interested. Plus, I don't know. This probably sounds mad, but, I mean … I haven't really got another, like, talent, have I? I watch all these people, like Beckham and all them. And they're entitled to make money out of what they are born with. Up until I met Robbie, Rachel's boyfriend, what I had had never done anything for me. And I thought, What's the difference? What's the difference between, I don't know, having a … having what I've got and being able to play the piano?"

"What's the difference?" said Dave. "You can't see what the difference is?"

"No," said Mark. "Tell me."

"Having a big thing isn't a talent, is it? Playing the piano is hard. I mean, what you've got doesn't … you know. It's not hard. It doesn't give people pleasure."

Mark and I stared at the carpet. I was trying not to laugh. Everything sounded like a Benny Hill joke. Eventually Dave caught on. And it didn't make things better. It could have been one of those moments that you see on TV, when everyone starts to laugh together. And the laughter would make the problem seem smaller than it had before. But Dave just lost his rag.

"It's not bloody funny."

"No one is laughing," I said.

"You were trying not to."

"I don't know what more we can do. We aren't laughing at something you don't think is funny," I said.

"But you still saw the joke. I can't see the joke. My son is a porn star. Where is the joke in that?"

"I'm not a porn –"

"Whatever. You're a freak, Mark. Being a freak is not the same thing as having a talent." Dave was angry. But there is still no excuse, is there? You can't call your own kid a freak and expect him to take it on the chin.

"You know it's – what do you call it?" said Mark. "Hereditary."

He knew what he was doing. He must have guessed years ago that he and Dave didn't share the same problem. Otherwise it would have come up by now. Oh, for God's sake … People say that when men argue, what they are really arguing about is, 'Who has got the biggest?' And here were my two men, my husband and son, arguing about exactly that. Except there was no argument. I'm probably the only person in the world who has seen both of them. And there was no need for a tape measure, if you know what I mean. Mark won, hands down. (Is that dirty, "Hands down"? It sounds dirty, doesn't it? But I don't know what it would mean.)

"Yeah, well, you don't get it from me. Mine is normal. Isn't it, Carol?" said Dave.

"Normal? Is that what you call it?" I said.

It was just a little joke, an attempt to jolly everyone along. On any other evening no one would have taken offence. But this wasn't any other evening, and offence was taken. I wasn't even thinking about the size thing. I had forgotten for a split second what wasn't normal. So I didn't mean to suggest that Dave's was small. (It's not. It's … well, it's normal.) I just meant that it wasn't, I don't know, curved, or covered in green spots, or could talk. That sort of abnormal. Jokey abnormal, not opposite-of-Mark's abnormal. If I had thought it through, I wouldn't have said anything. If I had thought it through, I wouldn't have found myself in bed at one in the morning talking to Dave about an affair I had twenty-five years ago.

5

"You know that thing with Steve?" asked Dave.

"No," I said.

"Steve. Steve Laird. You know."

"Oh. Yeah."

It wasn't as though I was playing dumb. I don't think I have heard his name since we got married. But even so, it wasn't like he appeared in our bed that night out of the middle of nowhere. I can't explain it, but when Dave brought Steve up, it sort of made sense. There was sex in the air that night. And it was not safe sex, if you know what I mean. It wasn't the comfortable, enjoyable sex that Dave and I have. The sort of sex you don't even have to think about. The sex we had been talking about was a dark, scary sex. And it was as if Dave had converted it into the only thing he had to hand.

"Was that what it was about?" he asked me.

"What?" I said.

"That."

"What's that?"

"You know," Dave said.

"No."

"That. Normal. Not normal."

"Are you asking me whether your penis is too small? Or whether Steve had a bigger one than you?"

"Shut up," said Dave.

"OK, I will."

I listened to him breathing in the dark. I knew we weren't finished. It

39

wasn't much of an affair, really. I wasn't married, for a start. Although Dave and I were living together, and we were sort of engaged. I only slept with Steve two or three times. And the sex wasn't anything much. It certainly wasn't the point, although I don't exactly remember what the point was. Something to do with feeling I was in a rut? And I know that Dave was in two minds about everything. He was flirting with this girl at work. He said it never went anywhere, but I was never quite sure …

"Yeah," he said about five minutes later.

"Yeah what?"

"Yeah, that's what I'm asking."

"Of course it wasn't about that. You know it wasn't," I said.

"Right."

"And I can't answer the other

question. Not because the answer would upset you. It's because I can't remember. You know it doesn't matter, don't you?" I asked.

"Yeah. Well, I know that's what you are supposed to say, anyway."

"It's the truth. It's like, I don't know. It wouldn't have mattered if he was taller than you or not."

"It would have mattered if I had been five foot and he had been six foot," said Dave.

"Yeah. But five foot is pretty small. You're not small like that, are you?"

"Oh, so what am I small like?"

"You're not small. For Christ's sake, Dave. You are smaller than your son. But I have seen your son. And, believe me, you wouldn't want to be like him either. Neither would I want you to be like him. Oh, and Steve wasn't like him either."

"You just said you couldn't re-member."

"You think I wouldn't remember something like that? Blimey. If he had been like Mark I would have had to talk to one of those therapists people see after disasters."

"I'm sorry," said Dave. I love Dave for lots of reasons. One of them is that he always knows when he is making an idiot of himself. "It's been a strange evening, though, hasn't it?"

I laughed. "You could say that, yes."

"What are we going to do?" he asked.

"I'm not sure we can do anything. It's his life. There are worse things to worry about."

"Are there?"

"Yeah. Of course. Drugs. Violence. All that stuff."

"Porn is like drugs, though, isn't it?

I mean, they are both a menace to society," Dave said.

"Put it this way. All those nights we have lain here listening for him to come home late at night … You worry if he has been stabbed, or if he is taking crack, or if he is driving home drunk. But have you ever stayed awake worrying he has been making a porno film?"

"No. But that's because I never thought of it before," Dave said.

"Yeah, and why didn't you think of it?"

"I don't know. I never thought he had it in him."

"That's not it. You never thought of it because it couldn't kill him. If it could have killed him, I would have thought about it, because I've thought about everything else," I said.

"What about AIDS?"

I got up, put my dressing-gown on, and hammered on Mark's door.

"What?" he said.

"What about AIDS?"

"Go to bed."

"No. Not until you have talked to me," I said.

"I'm not going into any details. But I'm not daft."

"You had better give me a few more details than that. That's not good enough."

"Thanks a bunch. There is absolutely nothing to worry about."

"I just want to say one more thing," said Dave when I had gone back to bed.

"Go on."

"Just one more thing about Mark's – you know. His talent."

"If you must."

"If it's hereditary ... It must have

been your dad."

My dad … Jesus.

I hope this never happens to you. But when you get your dad's thing and your son's thing dangled in your face, all on the same day … Well, you can imagine. It is not the sort of day you never want to end.

I went to sleep all right, though. Because for some reason that I can't, and don't really want to, explain, Dave and I ended up having sex that night. And it wasn't the sort of sex we usually have. It was more his idea than mine, but, you know. I joined in.

6

My mum lives with my sister Helen a couple of miles away. It is just one of those things that happened. Helen got divorced soon after Dad died. And she has never had any kids. It just seemed like a happy solution for everyone – especially, if I'm honest, for me and Dave. Helen moans about it a bit to me. She tries to make me feel guilty and so on. But the arrangement suits her, really. It's not like Mum's a geriatric. She is only sixty-eight. She is pretty fit, and she goes out a lot. She

goes out more than Helen, in fact.
Helen says that Mum stops her from
meeting anyone. But the only way that
could be is if Mum is actually copping
off with the men Helen is interested in.

I went around to see them on the
Saturday morning. I bumped into
Karen on the way to the bus stop. She
just happened to be putting her
recycling out the very moment I
walked past her front door. And if you
believe that, you will believe anything.

"So," she said.

"Hello, Karen." I gave her a big
smile.

"Did you watch it?"

"Oh, I've seen it all before," I said.
"Did Carl enjoy it?"

She looked at me. "He wasn't
looking at Mark, you know."

"Oh, of course not. I'm sure he will
get a girlfriend soon enough."

"And does he get it off his dad?"

"Have you ever wondered why I'm always so cheerful?" I said. And then I just kept walking.

I hadn't made up my mind if I was going to try and talk to Mum. We have never had that kind of conversation before. And once you get to a certain age, you are tempted to think that you've got away with it, aren't you? But it just seemed important. When Dad died, I went through the business of regretting that I hadn't spent enough time talking to him. I loved him. But I seemed to spend a lot of time resenting him, trying to avoid him, and getting pissed off with him. And now I was trying to work out if this business was something I should know about. Was it a part of him? And if so, was it a good part or a bad part?

Dad was really sick for the last couple of years of his life. Sick is how I remembered him best. But when I found out about this other thing, I started to think about him in a different way. I don't mean I started to think about him, you know, in an odd way. It's just that, knowing what I knew, I thought about him being young and healthy – or younger, anyway. It just seemed to follow. Because finding out something like that … You can't help but wonder about a period in his life when he would have been using it, if you know what I mean. And he couldn't have been using it much at the end, poor sod. And it really helped me to think about him in these other ways. I started to remember other things, like the way he dressed when Helen and I were kids. He dressed in trousers, like Mark, even though he was young in the sixties and seventies, when people were wearing tighter trousers. And on the bus that morning, I suddenly had a flash of the way he looked at my mum sometimes. And the way she looked at him. I'll tell you the truth. I suddenly got all weepy, on the top of the bus. I was sad, but it wasn't just sadness. There was something else in there too. It was that happy-and-sad, sweet-and-sour feeling you can get when you look at baby photos of your grown-up kids. I don't know. When you get older, it feels like happy memories and sad memories are pretty much the same thing. It is all just emotion in the end. And any of it can make you weep. Anyway, when I had dabbed at my eyes a bit, I almost started to laugh. Who would have thought that what began with Karen dropping a porn film through the letter box would end up with that sort of stuff going through your head?

7

Mum wasn't in, but Helen was.

"When will she be back?" I asked.

"She has only gone down to get her fags," Helen said. "I've stopped her smoking in here. Did I tell you? She has to go outside."

"You'll kill her," I said. It was only a joke. But you can't really joke with Helen.

"Oh, right. I'll kill her, not the fags."

"Yeah. Ironic, isn't it?"

She made me a cup of coffee. We sat down at the kitchen table.

"So what's new? I could do with some gossip," Helen said.

I laughed. I couldn't help it.

"What?" she asked.

"I don't know. Gossip."

"What about it?"

"People never really have any, do they? People always say, 'Got any gossip?' But if they have to ask, it means there isn't any. Because if there is any, they come out with it straight away."

I didn't know where I was going with this. I didn't know how much I wanted to say.

"So what you're saying is you've got nothing to tell me," she said.

"Not really."

And that was the moment I decided to tell her. I decided just when I had told her that I had nothing to tell her. It just seemed like too good an opportunity to miss. I get on OK with

Helen. But she can be really prissy. I suddenly saw that she would find out anyway, sooner or later. And I knew I would always regret not telling her myself, because I could choose the best moment. And the best moment was the moment she was least expecting it. I wanted the look on her face to be something I would remember forever. I wanted it to be something I would be describing to Dave, and maybe even Mark, over and over again.

"One funny thing, I suppose," I said. "Karen dropped this porn film through the door. You'll never guess who is in it."

She was already making this fantastic face, as if she was being choked by an invisible hand. She was going all pop-eyed and purple. I could have left it at that, and she would have needed to take deep breaths for the rest of the day.

"Do you want to know?" I said after a while, when she still hadn't said anything.

"Go on," she said.

"Mark," I said. "Our Mark. Your nephew."

"What do you mean, 'in a porn film'?"

"What do you think I mean? What else could I mean, other than what I've just said? When people say that Hugh Grant is in *Love, Actually*, what do they mean?" I said.

"*Love, Actually* isn't a porn film, though, is it?"

"What difference does that make?"

"I don't know. When you say that a famous actor is in a film, you're not saying very much. Are you? I mean, there's nothing that's difficult to understand. But when you tell me that my nephew is in a porn film ... I thought for a moment there was

54

something I wasn't getting. That you were using some slang I had never heard before," said Helen.

I wanted to laugh at her. But I couldn't laugh at that, because I knew what she meant. It was sort of what I felt when I saw the cover of the video. I felt that there was something about the photo that wasn't in my language, or wasn't aimed at my age group. I feel that way sometimes when Mark is watching that comedy programme when the man dressed as a woman says, "Yeah, but, no, but ..." And he just starts laughing.

Now that I think about it, this whole thing with Mark is like an episode of *Little Britain*, because I don't know whether it's funny or not.

"No," I said. "That's what I'm saying. Mark is in a porn film, like Hugh Grant was in *Love, Actually*. It turns out he has got a huge penis, and, and ..."

Helen was staring at me, trying hard to listen, trying hard to understand.

"I suppose he didn't know what to do with it," she said. "I suppose there isn't much you can do with it, if you think about it."

"You could just leave it in your trousers," I said.

"Well, yes. There is that. You weren't going to tell Mum, were you?"

"I don't know. I don't know why I came, really. Except the penis thing is supposed to be hereditary, and Dave hasn't got it. I mean, he has just got a normal one."

"Well, Mum hasn't … Oh, my God. You mean Dad?" said Helen.

"Yes."

"But he didn't … He couldn't have."

"Why not? I don't know. Do you?" I asked.

"No. God. Of course I don't. No.

God. Are you just going to come out and ask her?"

"I don't know. I'll see what I feel like when she gets back."

8

Mum came in, sat down, and took the plastic wrap off her cigarettes. Then, with a sigh and a little mutter, she remembered that she had to go outside.

"I'll come out with you," I said.

"You can have one here," said Helen.

"Why?"

"Lynn doesn't come over that often. I don't want to have to look at her through the window."

But she was worried that she was

going to miss something. You could tell. She took a saucer off the draining board and put it down on the table, for the ash.

"Did Dad ever smoke?" I asked Mum. It was a start. Maybe he always liked a fag after sex. It would be a short step from talking about that to asking her if …

"No," she said.

"Never?"

"I don't know about never. But he never smoked when he was with me. And he hated me smoking. Always on at me to give up. I wish I had. For him, I mean. He never asked for much. And I wouldn't even give him that."

She stubbed her cigarette out in disgust, half smoked. It was as if she were giving up now, four years too late.

"He only nagged because he was worried about you," I said. "As it happens, there was nothing to worry about. You're still with us, and you're still fagging away."

But there was no joking her out of it. Her eyes were glistening. All we could do now was drag her back and away from that horrible, dark, deep pit that she fell into after Dad died. Who was I to push her back into it? I changed the subject. We ended up talking about things that none of us could get upset about. We talked about why Mum won't use the halal butcher. We talked about whether *Big Brother* is a fake. (Helen has a thing about that.) And we talked about the family, including Mark. I told Mum he was ticking along. Helen caught my eye. And I thought she was going to giggle. But there's no joke in "ticking along", is there? Where's the pun in that?

Mark had a baby brother for about two hours on the morning of 5 June 1984.

We called him Nicky. He was born with a heart defect, and he died in an incubator, without ever being quite alive. I'm over it now. Of course I am. I was over it within a year or two. But I thought of the baby when I saw my mum struggling with the memory of my dad. And it wasn't just because of the grief, but because I could see how lucky I was. I am forty-nine years old, and those two deaths, Nicky's and my dad's, were the worst days of my life. Nothing else has even come close. What else would there be? Dave had a car accident and broke his arm. Mark got scarlet fever when he was little. But they were frightening for a moment or two, not devastating. And Mark's film career didn't even matter as much as either of the frightening things. I have been disappointed loads and loads of times. Who hasn't? But I wasn't even entirely sure that Mark's new career was disappointing. Like I said, it might even have been funny. And something that could be funny … Well, that's a whole different category. If you think that something might be funny, looked at in the right way, then look at it in the right way.

On the bus going home, I thought about what had happened since I found out that Mark was in a porn video. And what I realised was, all of it was good. The conversation I had with Dave about Steve was tricky, for a while. But then we ended up having really great sex. I really enjoyed being cheeky to Karen. On the bus going to Mum's, I'd had that little cry. And even that was because of being able to swap some miserable memories for some happy ones. Then there was that nice cup of coffee with Mum and Helen. And that would never have happened if I hadn't decided, for reasons best known to myself, to try and find out how big my father's thing was. Yes, looking at all that had happened, I can honestly say that it's an experience I could recommend to anyone. Can that be right?

9

Mark was making himself some lunch when I got back. He was frying up what looked like half a pound of bacon.

"Well," I said. "Someone is starving."

He looked at me. "Yeah. I am. But not because I've done anything, if that's what you mean."

"That's not what I meant. Calm down. Not everything I say is going to be about that."

"Sorry," he said.

I watched him make a mess of

turning the bacon over. So I took the wooden spatula thing from him.

"Do bad things happen to the girls in those films?" I asked.

"How do you mean?"

"Are they, I don't know, all on drugs, or on the game, or something?"

"No. That one I was … The one you saw, Vicky. She's a travel agent. She just got fed up with her breasts, the way I got fed up with … me. There's a few that want to do topless modelling. But that's about it. Rachel's boyfriend, he loves making films. He wants to be Steven Spielberg. And this is about as close as he can get for the moment."

"He's rubbish," I said. "He makes *Carry On* look like *Dances with Wolves* or something."

"He's terrible," said Mark. "I don't want to stop, Mum."

"Oh. Why not?"

"It doesn't make any difference, you and Dad finding out. I wasn't doing it because I could get away with it, you know."

"So how long do you want to do it for?" I asked.

"I don't know. Till I'm on my feet, I suppose."

"Make me a promise." I didn't know what I wanted from him until I said it. But when I came out with it it sounded right. "Stop when something worse happens."

"What does that mean?" he asked.

"You know. When, I don't know … When your gran dies. Or when your dad and I get divorced or something. Stop then."

"Why do you say that?"

"I don't know. It just feels right," I said.

"But shouldn't it be the other way around? I mean, when something bad happens you won't notice this," he said.

"No. But I'll know it's there, that's the thing. I don't want to know it's there when I don't feel the same as I do now."

"How do you feel now?" he asked.

"I feel OK. That's the thing."

He shrugged. "All right, then. I promise. Unless you know for a fact you're getting divorced in the next week or so."

"No, we are all right for the time being."

He reached out his hand and we shook. "Deal," he said, and we left it at that.

That night, the three of us went out to the Crown for a drink before our dinner. We used to do it quite a lot when Mark was in his late teens. Then it was a novelty for us all. But soon

Mark found better things to do, and we stopped. It wasn't like this huge thing. We didn't all decide that we should spend quality time together in order to get to know one another better. It just happened. Dave said he fancied going out for a drink. And Mark and I were in the same sort of mood. But I was glad that somehow the film had moved us back in time, rather than forward. I was glad that we had somehow ended up doing something we used to do. It needn't have been that way.

Anyway, I had this strange moment. Admittedly, I'd been drinking lager on an empty stomach. Dave was getting the drinks in. Mark was playing on the fruit machine. Then it was as if I floated out of myself and saw the three of us, all in our different places, all looking cheerful. And I thought, I would have settled for this on just about any day of my life since Nicky died. I wouldn't have settled for it before I got married. But you don't know then, do you? You don't know how scared you will feel or how many compromises you will make. You don't know that just about anything that looks OK on the outside can be made to feel OK on the inside. You don't know that it has to work that way around.

OPEN DOOR SERIES

order details overleaf

TRADE/CREDIT CARD ORDERS TO:
CMD, 55A Spruce Avenue,
Stillorgan Industrial Park,
Blackrock, Co. Dublin, Ireland.
Tel: (+353 1) 294 2560
Fax: (+353 1) 294 2564

TO PLACE PERSONAL/EDUCATIONAL
ORDERS OR TO ORDER A CATALOGUE
PLEASE CONTACT:
New Island, 2 Brookside,
Dundrum Road, Dundrum,
Dublin 14, Ireland.
Tel: (+353 1) 298 6867/298 3411
Fax: (+353 1) 298 7912
www.newisland.ie